HUG O' WAR

HELL @ WAR

HUG O' WAR

Handwritten Poems and Memoirs and
Graphological Profiles of successful people
in various occupations

Conceived & compiled by
Janna Spark

Quartet Books

First published by Quartet Books Limited in 2000
A member of the Namara Group
27 Goodge Street
London W1P 2LD

This collection copyright © Janna Spark 2000
An extension of the copyright page can be found on p. 289

Cover illustration from *The Bear* by Raymond Briggs, published by Red
Fox. Reproduced by kind permission of the artist and The Random House
Archive & Library

A catalogue record for this book is available from the British Library

ISBN 0 7043 8144 3

Phototypeset by FiSH Books, London
Printed and bound in Finland by WS Bookwell

Dedicated to the children of Kosovo for whose
benefit this book is being published

HUG O' WAR

In hug o' war
There is no struggle:
Everyone wins
The warmth of a huggle.

There is no hate, no deadly fate,
No bitter tears, no lifelong fears,
No shattered souls nor hearts with holes.
No haunted corners, screaming fears,
No need to block those bitter tears.

In hug o' war
There is no struggle:
Everyone wins
The warmth of a huggle.

Janna Spark

CONTENTS

ACKNOWLEDGEMENTS

The *Hug O'War* book was like a chain-letter of goodwill: it would never have happened without the support of a great many people – both children and adults – each of whom tried to reach someone they knew to participate and all of whom deserve to be recognised for their effort. In particular, my husband, **Iko Meshoulam**, who, with indefatigable energy and commitment to this cause, spent countless hours with letter writing, legal documents, meetings, shuttling and delivering urgent parcels and proofreading.

Many thanks to:
- each of the participants, for their heartfelt contributions.
- the British Academy of Graphology research team: Kay Goulandris, Sarah Mooney, Tony Soar, Monique Sterling, and Savina Serpieri, Head of Research.
- the Society of Authors, and in particular, Mark LeFanu and Elaine Kidd.
- Naim Attallah who took less than fifteen minutes to agree to publish *Hug O'War*.
- Noam and Geraldine Gottesman whose immediate and generous financial donation made the publication of *Hug O'War* possible.

- Aron Gelbard, whose invitation for me to participate at the study-day at his school triggered the idea of doing this project in the first place.
- Alex Kissin, who helped decide on the questions to put to the participants.
- Max Gainza, who gave up Saturday rowing to help with selecting and recording sources of poems, to be quite literally my writing hand.
- Daphne Astor, for her many wise and always insightful suggestions.

I would also like to thank the following people for helping to contact possible participants, procuring contact addresses, lending poetry books, finding and selecting poems:

Micky Astor	Morris Berman	Shirley Berman
Julie Betteridge	Peter Boddington	Anna Boglione
Gail Boglione	Molly Bown	Georgina Bullough
Jessica Chappatte	Smadar Cohen	Clare Conville
Bruce Dundas	Sophie Dundas	Annette Ellis
Kay Goulandris	Dianne Hofmeyr	Barbara Kean
Soussie Kerman	Ann Leach	Sarah McDougall
Casper MacKenzie	Felix MacKenzie	Barbara Manfrey
Elizabeth Miles	Laura Miles	Cao Neto
George Norman	Lizzy Plapinger	Maryam Sachs
Nick Scott	Joseph West	Sara Woodhatch

INTRODUCTION

This book contains
- a collection of childrens' poems, handwritten by well-known successful people in various occupations
- handwritten responses of these people to one of the following requests:
    (i) write about why you chose your particular career; or
    (ii) write about a memorable moment in your childhood
- handwriting analysis of each participant specifically looking at characteristics that make this particular person successful.

These handwritings were analysed by members of the British Academy of Graphology. It was thought appropriate to concentrate uniquely on those personality elements relevant to the writer's occupation and the success they have made of it. Consequently, it should be emphasised that these portraits are not in-depth analyses.

THE STORY BEHIND
THE BOOK

At around the height of the Kosovo conflict, I received an invitation to speak at a special study day organised at a London day school, where the central theme was '*identity*'. In my lecture I addressed the question: why certain people are successful at their particular chosen career and examined with the students detailed graphological profiles of some of the participants. This served as the launching pad for the Hug O'War idea: a project to raise money for the children of the war-torn Kosovo area. It made a perfect circle: the chance to reach both those children with a bright future ahead of them and other children with a grim present and uncertain future.

Originally it was going to be just a poetry book for children. On one side there would be the handwritten version of a poem, perhaps with an autograph signature, and on the opposite page would be the printed text of that poem. This would ensure easy reading, in case someone's handwriting was illegible.

Handwritten copied poems would not be sufficient for a proper graphological analysis, as these are structured and do not produce spontaneous writing.

So each participant was also asked to answer one of two questions that would induce spontaneous writing. This spontaneous sample initially was not intended for the book, but solely for the graphological research.

However, when the spontaneous writings came in, each very touching or funny or precious in its own way, I realised that these had to be included in the book, together with the graphological analysis.

It is hoped that this book will bring pleasure to the reader, old or young, whilst at the same time the funds raised from this project will bring some comfort to the suffering children of Kosovo.

London, 2000   Janna Spark

HUG O' WAR

FARAD AFSHAR

Consultant Neurosurgeon

The Eagle.

Alfred, Lord Tennyson. (1809–1892)

He clasps the crag with crooked hands;
close to the sun in lonely lands,
Ring'd with the azure world, he stands.

The wrinkled sea beneath him crawls;
He watches from his mountain walls.
And like a thunderbolt he falls.

THE EAGLE

He clasps the crag with crookèd hands;
Close to the sun in lonely lands,
Ring'd with the azure world, he stands.

The wrinkled sea beneath him crawls;
He watches from his mountain walls,
And like a thunderbolt he falls.

Alfred, Lord Tennyson (1809–1892)

A memorable moment in my childhood.

I was five years old - mid afternoon - northern
Iran, Russian border at my grand parents
home. I was taken for a walk outside the
house - peace & tranquility. Suddenly
Russian tanks seem to ramble down the street.
    I was pushed back into the house & told
that no one must venture out of doors between
5.0 pm & the next morning or they may get shot
    Even at that age I was aware of a gross
infringement of one's liberty & the intense
fear that I experienced for the 1st time in
my life.

                              F. Afshar   .

A memorable moment in my childhood.

I was five years old – mid afternoon – Northern Iran,
Russian border at my grandparents' home. I was taken
for a walk outside the house – peace and tranquillity.
Suddenly Russian tanks seem to rumble down the
street. I was pushed back into the house and told that
no one must venture out of doors between 5.00pm
and the next morning or they may get shot. Even at
that age I was aware of a gross infringement of one's
liberty and the intense fear that I experienced for the
first time in my life.

F. AFSHAR

Single-minded, with a taste for action, he never loses sight of his goals and will persevere until they have been reached. He has drive, purposefulness and efficiency. Results are what matter to him and he forges ahead with ardour and enthusiasm for the task at hand.

He has good foresight and shows discipline and initiative. His thinking is deductive, systematic and logical, supported by traditional values.

This is a caring man, whose morals give him integrity, rectitude and sincerity. He has a warm sociable personality and enjoys the contact of his fellow beings.

2

NAIM ATTALLAH

Publisher

Going to St. Ives

As I was going to St. Ives
I met a man with seven wives.
Every wife had seven sacks,
Every sack had seven cats,
Every cat had seven kits.
Kits, cats, sacks, and wives,
How many were going to St Ives?

GOING TO ST. IVES

As I was going to St. Ives
I met a man with seven wives.
Every wife had seven sacks,
Every sack had seven cats,
Every cat had seven kits.
Kits, cats, sacks, and wives,
How many were going to St. Ives?

Traditional

A memorable moment of my childhood.

As a child I was sent to live with my grandmother in Nazareth, a safe haven from the hostilities in Palestine. She was a simple woman whose wisdom came from nature and the land on which she grew fruit and vegetables. All the magic and enchantment of that formative period in my life were bound up with my love for that wonderful old woman. One day, as we tilled the soil together, she took up some earth in her hand and let it run through her fingers. "This is what feeds us," she said "and what allows us to live." That moment together taught me the deep significance of land, symbolic and actual. It is something I have never forgotten.

N. Attallah

A memorable moment of my childhood.

As a child I was sent to live with my grandmother in Nazareth, a safe haven from the hostilities in Palestine. She was a simple woman whose wisdom came from nature and the land on which she grew fruit and vegetables. All the magic and enchantment of that formative period in my life were bound up with my love for that wonderful old woman. One day, as we tilled the soil together, she took up some earth in her hand and let it run through her fingers. "This is what feeds us," she said, "and what allows us to live." That moment together taught me the deep significance of land, symbolic and actual. It is something I have never forgotten.

N . ATTALLAH

The writer is full of vitality, spontaneity and astuteness. He has an innate taste for action as well as warmth of personality and sensual enjoyment of life.

He is observant, critical, with a sharp and mobile mind that perceives possibilities that immediately provide ideas for realistic projects, which he wastes no time in putting into action.

His fertile imagination, enthusiasm and love for a challenge, combined with intuitive judgement, conviction and perseverance, make for a dynamic achiever who enriches not only his own life, but the lives of others as well.

He certainly is a man to be reckoned with, yet he is full of feelings and confident of the future.

3

DAVID BECKHAM

Professional Football Player

Hey diddle diddle
The cat had a fiddle
The cow jumped over the moon
The little dog laughed to see such sport
And the dish ran away with the spoon

HEY DIDDLE DIDDLE

Hey diddle diddle, the cat and the fiddle,
The cow jumped over the moon;
The little dog laughed
To see such fun,
And the dish ran away with the spoon.

Traditional

The most memorable moment in my childhood, was when I played on the right hand wing for Waltham Forest Under 12's against Redbridge. It was one of my best games for the district. My mum called me over (my dad was working) there was excitement in her voice, when she said 'Its lucky you had a good game, because there was a scout from Man United and he wants to talk to dad to discuss taking you to the club for trials, I leapt into the air and started to cry. It was a dream come true. The rest is now history of my good fortune. at Manchester United

The most memorable moment in my childhood, was when I played on the right hand wing for Waltham Forest Under 12s against Redbridge. It was one of my best games for the district, my mum called me over (my dad was working) there was excitement in her voice, when she said, 'It's lucky you had a good game, because there was a scout from Man United and he wants to talk to dad to discuss taking you to the club for trials.' I leapt into the air and started to cry. It was a dream come true. The rest is now history – my good fortune at Manchester United.

DAVID BECKHAM

This is a disciplined young man with ambition, enthusiasm and high aspirations. There is a need for self-affirmation and he likes to feel included amongst others. He has concern for rules and principles, a good co-ordination of ideas and actions, and a sense of space. This all stands him in good stead as a dedicated member of a team.

His straightforward youthful outlook, open mind and adaptability impart a capacity to learn and develop further, without side issues and distractions throwing him off course. Occasionally his natural enthusiasm may tend to overreach his available energy, but in general his prudence and self-control enable him to marshal his resources to advantage.

Although perhaps not yet sufficiently self-assured to feel comfortable as a leader of others he nonetheless carries a certain authority by virtue of the integrity, imagination and concentration with which he exercises his skills.

4

HELENA BONHAM CARTER

Actress

Caterpillar Serenade.

Rest and sleep come soon
After I weave my silk cocoon
Dreams of splendid things
And rainbow colours on my wings.

Eyes now closed
Curl up tight
For what is to be my longest night.

Heaven black
Heaven blue
Heaven please

Make all my dreams come true.

CATERPILLAR SERENADE

Rest and sleep come soon
After I weave my silk cocoon
Dreams of splendid things
And rainbow colours on my wings.
Eyes now closed
Curl up tight
For what is to be my longest night.
Heaven black
Heaven blue
Heaven please
Make all my dreams come true.

Janna Spark

I was a small child of five when
my mother suffered a nervous breakdown.
Everything that year assumed outlandish
proportions: our christmas tree loomed
eighteen feet above my mere three; I
could climb entirely into my christmas
stocking that was substantially longer
than my actual bed; as for the easter
eggs ... well only a dinasaur could have
laid them.
    I remember being somewhat disappointed
when she finally recovered and things
resumed a more normal size.

                    Helena Bonham Carter.

I was a small child of five when my mother suffered a nervous breakdown. Everything that year assumed outlandish proportions; our Christmas tree loomed eighteen feet above my mere three; I could climb entirely into my Christmas stocking that was substantially longer than my actual bed; as for the Easter eggs... well only a dinosaur could have laid them.

I remember being somewhat disappointed when she finally recovered and things resumed a more normal size.

HELENA BONHAM CARTER

HELENA BONHAM CARTER

This is a person with a receptive mind, a broad assimilation of ideas and a creative originality. There is an underlying practical realism that imparts a flexible adaptability without upsetting her equilibrium or compromising her integrity.

She has a natural ease of communication and an effortless consistency in the conduct of her affairs. Her own stability and an open and patient approach towards others enable her to reassure those around her. Receptive to colour and form she has a well developed aesthetic sense, which she exercises with a tasteful discretion. Showy flamboyance is not in her nature. Her attitudes are firm and supple, never brittle or rigid. She sees poetry in life.

5

WILLIAM BOYD

Novelist

"Mary had a little lamb"

Mary had a little lamb,
A lobster, and some prunes,
A glass of milk, a piece of pie,
And then some macaroons.

It made the busy waiters grin
To see her order so,
And when they carried Mary out
Her face was white as snow.

'MARY HAD A LITTLE LAMB'

Mary had a little lamb,
A lobster, and some prunes,
A glass of milk, a piece of pie,
And then some macaroons.

It made the busy waiters grin
To see her order so,
And when they carried Mary out,
Her face was white as snow.

Anon.

I wanted to be a writer because
I couldn't imagine myself being
anything else.

William Boyd

I wanted to be a writer because I couldn't imagine myself being anything else.

WILLIAM BOYD

The writer has a quick, penetrating, lucid and enquiring mind, receptive to new ideas, enabling him to understand people and situations. He has the intellectual discipline to be able to see essentials and yet take account of details.

A fine balance is maintained between intuition and deduction, which combined with inventiveness and aestheticism, makes for genuine creativity.

He is independent by nature, but communicates well, and is responsive to others.

Though emotionally sensitive, he would tend to keep his own feelings well under control, and might feel more at ease socially in an atmosphere of intellectual exchange than one of cosy personal contact.

If and when his confidence might falter, he is able to rely on his intellectual drive, his strong sense of quality, ethical attitude and self-discipline.

With a predilection for matters of the mind, this is a mature, refined and evolved personality, aware of his importance in relation to the world about him. True autonomy has been reached.

6

SIR RICHARD BRIERS

Actor

The panther is like a leopard
Except it hasn't been peppered.
Should you behold a panther crouch
Prepare to say Ouch.
Better yet, if called by a panther
Don't anther.

THE PANTHER

The panther is like a leopard
Except it hasn't been peppered.
Should you behold a panther crouch,
Prepare to say Ouch.
Better yet, if called by a panther,
Don't anther.

Ogden Nash

The greatest joy for me is getting
a really good laugh from an
audience. Over the last decade,
thanks to Kenneth Branagh I have
broadened my range of parts in
Shakespeare. I have now become
a respected all round Actor —
been I do miss the laughs!

Richard Briers

The greatest joy for me is getting a really good laugh from an audience. Over the last decade, thanks to Kenneth Branagh I have broadened my range of parts in Shakespeare. I have now become a respected all round Actor – but I do miss the laughs!

RICHARD BRIERS

This man is vivacious and versatile and able to grasp opportunities coming his way. He has resilience and plays life as it comes. Disliking routine, he is stimulated by new ideas and projects, and adapts quickly.

He has warmth with people, humour and easy communication on a social level with an underlying defensive caution.

His thinking is intuitive and imaginative rather than highly organised or dryly intellectual.

His ambition is directed more towards present activity than striving towards a distant goal. He remains independent following his own tastes and desires.

7

RAYMOND BRIGGS

Writer & Illustrator

maggy and milly and molly and may
went down to the beach to play one day

and maggie discovered a shell that sang
so sweetly she couldn't remember her troubles, and

milly befriended a stranded star
whose rays five languid fingers were;

and molly was chased by a horriblething
which raced sideways while blowing bubbles: and

may come home with a smooth round stone
as small as a world and as large as alone.

For whatever we lose (like a you or a me)
it's always ourselves we find in the sea.

E. E. Cummings

MAGGIE AND MILLY
AND MOLLY AND MAY

maggie and milly and molly and may
went down to the beach (to play one day)

and maggie discovered a shell that sang
so sweetly she couldn't remember her troubles, and

milly befriended a stranded star
whose rays five languid fingers were;

and molly was chased by a horrible thing
which raced sideways while blowing bubbles: and

may came home with a smooth round stone
as small as a world and as large as alone.

For whatever we lose (like a you or a me)
it's always ourselves we find in the sea

E. E. Cummings

Ron, a seven-year-old evacuee in 1940, said to me: "Your aunties don't know everything."

This was a revelation to me. I was five at the time and I suddenly realised that adults could be fallible, did not know everything and were not perfect. I might know something they did not. They could be wrong, I might be right!

Raymond Briggs
7 May 99

Ron, a seven-year-old evacuee in 1940, said to me: 'Your aunties don't know everything.'

This was a revelation to me. I was five at the time and I suddenly realised that adults could be fallible, did not know everything and were not perfect. I might know something they did not. *They* could be wrong, *I* might be right!

RAYMOND BRIGGS

A clear and creative mind, responsive to the world of form, colour and texture, the writer has talent for expressiveness and depth of feeling.

He is sympathetic and has a warm sociability and generosity. He enjoys communication, which does not preclude some reserve and unostentatious dignity.

Thoughtful, reflective and logical, he approaches his work in a simple and direct manner, using his sensual aestheticism to express himself.

He is serious, well organised in his activities and pays attention to details. He works steadily with concentration and patience and is not easily deflected from his goals which he pursues with quiet confidence.

Traditional in his outlook, he has firm moral values, whilst retaining flexibility. He conducts himself with self-control and resistance to influence.

8

SIMON CALLOW

Actor

A Slash of Blue

A slash of Blue —
A sweep of Gray —
Some scarlet patches on the way,
Compose an Evening Sky —
A little purple — slipped between.
Some Ruby Trousers hurried on —
A Wave of Gold —
A Bank of Day —
That just makes out the Morning Sky.

Emily Dickinson (1830 - 1886)

A SLASH OF BLUE

A slash of Blue –
A sweep of Gray –
Some scarlet patches on the way,
Compose an Evening Sky –
A little purple – slipped between
Some Ruby Trousers hurried on –
A Wave of Gold –
A Bank of Day –
This just makes out the Morning Sky.

Emily Dickinson

I'm living in Africa - in Zambia: in the small town of Fort Jameson - and I'm nine years old. It's Christmas; the school concert. People sing songs, do sketches. I've been deputed to read the Gospel narrative of the Nativity. I am disgracefully, unforgivably restless during everyone else's pieces. All the performers are sitting on the stage in a line, and my fidgeting is impossible to ignore. Finally I stand up to read, to an audience that must hate me. But after 30 seconds, I have them eating out of my hand. At the end, quite inappropriately, they applaud. This is the moment at which I became an actor.

Simon Callow

I'm living in Africa – in Zambia, in the small town of Fort Jameson – and I'm nine years old. It's Christmas; the school concert. People sing songs, do sketches. I've been deputed to read the Gospel narrative of the nativity. I am disgracefully, unforgivably restless during everyone else's pieces. All the performers are sitting on the stage in a line, and my fidgeting is impossible to ignore. Finally I stand up to read, to an audience that must hate me. But after 30 seconds, I have them eating out of my hand. At the end, quite inappropriately, they applaud. This is the moment at which I became an actor.

SIMON CALLOW

A rich, colourful personality, the writer has a restless energy and enthusiasm combined with a need for social contacts and for recognition.

Self-discipline, perfectionism and a perceptive sense of style give direction to his creativity and help to override any inhibitions or lapses in self-confidence that may get in the way of goals.

Similarly his vivid imagination, sensitivity and warmth of feeling are matched by a self-possession, realism and ironic view of life, so that he manages to avoid a confusion of priorities.

With his independent, intuitive and sharp intelligence, he has an original outlook. Perseverance and courage play a part in the achievement of his ambition.

9

PAUL CARTLEDGE

Professor of Greek History,
Cambridge University

TREES

The Oak is called the King of Trees,
The Aspen quivers in the breeze,
The Poplar grows up straight and tall,
The Pear-tree spreads along the wall,
The Sycamore gives pleasant shade,
The Willow droops in watery glade,
The Fir-tree useful timber gives,
The Beech amid the forest lives.

Sara Coleridge

TREES

The Oak is called the King of Trees,
The Aspen quivers in the breeze,
The Poplar grows up straight and tall,
The Pear-tree spreads along the wall,
The Sycamore gives pleasant shade,
The Willow droops in watery glade,
The Fir-tree useful timber gives,
The Beech amid the forest lives.

Sara Coleridge

Aged eight, I was reading a simplified 'Told to The Children' version of the Odyssey, in bed or at any rate my bedroom in Putney. I reached the point in the story where Odysseus, disguised as a beggar by his protector-goddess Athene, returns at last after twenty years' absence to his palace on Ithaca. No one recognises him. More accurately, no <u>human</u> recognises him. But Argos does. Poor old Argos, blind, tick-ridden, mangey, once the swiftest hound in Odysseus's hunting pack, but now condemned to eke out his days miserably amid the palace dung-heaps. Recognition of his master was too much for his ancient heart — he rolled over and died from the mingled joy and shock. Odysseus wept a surreptitious tear. I howled, for half an hour solid. This, I like to think, was the beginning of my interest in and love for Classics.

Paul Cartledge

Aged eight, I was reading a simplified 'Told to the Children' version of the *Odyssey*, in bed or at any rate in my bedroom in Putney. I reached the point in the story where Odysseus, disguised as a beggar by his protector-goddess Athene, returns at last after twenty years' absence to his palace on Ithaca. No one recognises him. More accurately, no <u>human</u> recognises him. But Argos does. Poor old Argos, blind, tick-ridden, mangey, once the swiftest hound in Odysseus's hunting pack, but now condemned to eke out his days miserably amid the palace dung-heaps. Recognition of his master was too much for his ancient heart – he rolled over and died from the mingled joy and shock. Odysseus wept a surreptitious tear. I howled for half an hour solid. This, I like to think, was the beginning of my interest in and love for Classics.

PAUL CARTLEDGE

The writer has an unusually strong vitality which is used to make a mark on the world.

He has mental flexibility, agility and speed, with the ability to see the essential and to take a general view of situations. He can criticise, analyse and synthesise, with prudence and objectivity.

Not so much an aggressive authoritarian, he nevertheless has firm attitudes and commands respect due to his competence and charisma.

He has principles, a sense of ethics and duty as well as high standards on which he will not compromise. He has high aspirations, will power, self-control and would not like to be taken for granted.

Although sensitive, he has no time for sentimentality. An able and active man, he likes to be recognised for his achievements.

10

BRIAN CLARKE

Artist

How doth the little crocodile
Improve his shining tail;
And pour the waters of the Nile
On every golden scale!

How cheerfully he seems to grin,
How neatly spreads his claws,
And welcomes little fishes in,
With gently smiling jaws!

HOW DOTH THE LITTLE CROCODILE

How doth the little crocodile
Improve his shining tail;
And pour the waters of the Nile
On every golden scale!

How cheerfully he seems to grin,
How neatly spreads his claws,
And welcomes little fishes in,
With gently smiling jaws!

Lewis Carroll

Dressing up in a "Beatle-jacket"
on Whit-sunday.

spianeeasne

Dressing up in a 'Beatle-jacket' on Whit-Sunday.

BRIAN CLARKE

This man has a strong sense of his own autonomy and of how things should be done. His aesthetic feel for colour, form and style demands stimulation and expression. To this is added a certain emotional warmth so that he enjoys operating in the field of social exchange and among people. However, he does not like what he would regard as messy involvement, so would endeavour, in day to day work, to maintain an emotional distance from others, on all but a practical level.

He is creative but realistic, so is able to keep a sensible rein on his imagination and is conscious of his own worth.

Disciplined and orderly, he instinctively maintains a measure of detachment from whatever enterprise for which he is responsible. He is thus better able to take an overall view and to feel in control, without needing to be rigid or authoritarian. In this way he is able to motivate others in an atmosphere of mutual co-operation on his own terms, and still maintain the standards he requires.

11

RICHARD CURTIS

Writer

Richard Curtis.

She Walks in Beauty

She walks in beauty, like the night
Of cloudless climes and starry skies;
And all that's best of dark and bright
Meet in her aspect and her eyes;
Thus mellowed to that tender light
Which heaven to gaudy day denies

George Gordon, Lord Byron.

SHE WALKS IN BEAUTY

She walks in beauty, like the night
Of cloudless climes and starry skies;
And all that's best of dark and bright
Meet in her aspect and her eyes:
Thus mellowed to that tender light
Which heaven to gaudy day denies.

George Gordon, Lord Byron

<u>Ronald Valentine?</u>

Two memorable moments that have
totally affected my adult life.

First, driving from the airport in Manila to
our comfy home in the suburbs, past
miles after mile of slums, thousands of
people living under corrugated iron roofs,
with no walls. Ever since then I've
known that every happy day I have is a tough,
tough day for other people — & that's why I do
Red Nose Day...

on the other hand — one cold October morning
in Sweden — sitting on the school bus, blithe &
normal. The bus stopped. on got a girl, in a
black polo neck & red skirt. within a few
seconds I was mad with love. Her name was
Tracy N. Thompson, her initials TNT, & surely
she blew my life apart. And that's why I write
those romantic movies, to make Tracy fall in love with me,
eventually.

Two memorable moments that have totally affected my adult life.

First, driving from the airport in Manila to our comfy home in the suburbs, past miles after mile of slums, thousands of people living under corrugated iron roofs, with no walls. Ever since then I've known that every happy day I have is a tough, tough day for other people – that's why I do Red Nose Day...

On the other hand – one cold October morning in Sweden – sitting on the school bus, blithe and normal. The bus stopped: on got a girl in a black polo neck + red skirt. Within ten seconds, I was mad with love. Her name was Tracy N. Thompson, her initials TNT, + surely she blew my life apart. And that's why I write those romantic movies, to make Tracey fall in love with me, eventually.

RICHARD CURTIS

RICHARD CURTIS

An exuberant vivacity of mind combined with a flair for communicating ideas enables this person to express his creativity in an original way.

An individualist, his enterprising spirit and lively imagination may tend to give rise to a certain impatience with imposed routine. However, his fertile, sharp, mobile mind and innate professionalism carry him successfully along in pursuit of goals in a manner which is more ad hoc than preplanned.

Independence of judgement, optimism and initiative reflect a confidence in his own sense of style.

He has an incisive wit that reflects his ability to reveal possibilities in situations which others may overlook and he rather enjoys the element of surprise.

Sociable rather than sentimental, he has an intuitive capacity for adapting to others whilst exercising his talents towards the fulfilment of his aspirations.

12

MARYAM D'ABO

Actress & Producer

Humpty Dumpty sat on a wall.
Humpty Dumpty had a great fell.
all the King's horses
And all the King's men
Couldn't put Humpty together again.

HUMPTY DUMPTY

Humpty Dumpty
Sat on the wall,
Humpty Dumpty
Had a great fall.
All the king's horses
And all the king's men
Couldn't put Humpty
Together again.

Traditional

I chose to be an actress because of the communication with people from all walks of life on a purely artistic level. All of us together telling a meaningful story exposed (hopefully) to the rest of the world —

I chose to be an actress because of the communication with people from all walks of life on a purely artistic level. All of us together telling a meaningful story expressed (hopefully) to the rest of the world.

MARYAM D'ABO

An individual who tends to evaluate life's situations through her emotions, she is intuitive and imaginative, rather than methodical and logical.

She has an artistic nature and needs attention. Her self-confidence varies but, given a frame of reference, she works well in a team. Alone, she is in constant quest to determine her ultimate goal.

She is also rather romantic and does become attached in relationships. She likes to please, though may feel hurt if this is not reciprocated.

She has a need for change and for physical activity.

13

ALAIN DE BOTTON

Writer

Six thirty
Seven thirty
Quarter to eight -

I hate to go to bed
when I'm feeling so great!

If I sweep the sky
And polish the stars
And dust the rust
Which covers Mars -

Pull the moon
By a string to make me stronger -

Could I please
Stay up a little longer?'

BEDTIME NEGOTIATIONS

Six thirty
Seven thirty
Quarter to eight –
I hate to go to bed
When I'm feeling so great!
If I sweep the sky
And polish the stars
And dust the rust
Which covers Mars–
Pull the moon
By a string to make me stronger–
Could I please
Stay up a little longer?

Janna Spark

Writing books seemed a way to live fully -
unless one thinks about what happens to one,
one sometimes misses out on the most crucial
aspects of experiences. Writing is is the perfect
way to reflect and to understand one's own
life.

Alain de Botton

Writing books seemed a way to live fully – unless one thinks about what happens to one, one sometimes misses out on the most crucial aspects of experiences. Writing is the perfect way to reflect and to understand one's own life.

ALAIN DE BOTTON

The writer is a very sensitive man with a contemplative nature. His thinking is mostly intuitive. He reflects and dreams a lot. His attitude to life is artistic; practical and material considerations are not of great interest to him. He is gentle and warm, but is rather shy in expressing his intimate feelings with a possible tendency to dwell at times on issues that deeply concern and affect him, but he can nevertheless see the funny side of life.

He is influenced by a rich inner life. He needs his freedom and time to contemplate. Mysticism and communion with nature are his gateways to expression, artistically manifested. It is through his writing that he is able to express himself and communicate his rich unconscious life.

14

J.P. DONLEAVY

Author

Jack And Jill

Jack and Jill went up the hill
  To fetch a pail of water;
Jack fell down, and broke his crown,
  And Jill came tumbling after.

Then up Jack got and off did trot,
    As fast as he could caper,
To old Dame Dob, who patched his
    nob
  With vinegar and brown paper.

JACK AND JILL

Jack and Jill went up the hill,
To fetch a pail of water;
Jack fell down and broke his crown,
And Jill came tumbling after.

Up Jack got and home did trot,
As fast as he could caper;
He went to bed to mend his head,
With vinegar and brown paper.

Traditional

A memorable moment of childhood
was sitting on a porch minded by an
older cousin of seraphic mien
who before I had to go to bed
let me wait until I'd seen
a shooting star. In the distance
the sound of waves on the
Sagaponack shore of Long
Island when it was once
all potato fields. And her
voice was sweet and her
nature patient when I'd say
I just want to see one more
shooting star.

J. P. Ambury

A memorable moment of childhood was sitting on a porch minded by an older cousin of seraphic mien who before I had to go to bed let me wait until I'd seen a shooting star. In the distance the sound of waves on the Sagaponack shore of Long Island when it was once all potato fields. And her voice was sweet and her nature patient when I'd say I just want to see one more shooting star.

J. P. DONLEAVY

This is a man with drive and ambition. He is able to combine logical reasoning with a spontaneous intuition and for him, there is a relatively easy interplay between the two apparent opposites. The result affords a productive channel for his creativity, especially as he is shrewd, perceptive, quick to grasp essentials and confident in his judgement.

He has an outgoing urge to explore and to extend his boundaries. His need for shared experience is modified by a tendency not to reveal to others too much of his own inner promptings, remaining rather aloof.

A sensitive man, he is self-motivated and, whilst keeping within the framework of traditional values, is wary of constraints imposed from without.

He can be tenacious, critical, and ironic – even combative if necessary – but he is not, by nature, an aggressive man.

Setting himself high standards, he takes a pride in what he does and this creates a certain tension which has driven him towards activity and work.

15

THEO FENNELL

Jewellery Designer

Two funny men.

I know a man,
Who's upside down,
And when he goes to bed
His head's not on the pillow. No!
His feet are there instead.

I know a man
Who's back to front,
The strangest man I've seen.
He can't tell where he's going
But he knows where he has been.

Spike Milligan.
— .. —

TWO FUNNY MEN

I know a man
Who's upside down,
And when he goes to bed
His head's not on the pillow. No!
His *feet* are there instead.

I know a man
Who's back to front,
The strangest man *I've* seen.
He can't tell where he's going
But he knows where he has been.

Spike Milligan

I wasn't lucky enough to choose
a career, as I have always been
unemployable, but fortunately these came
in a series of strange and
kismet-like ways. It ended up
being the only one of a series
of creative endeavours that I
could make a living out of —
failed poet, songwriter, musician,
writer, portrait-painter etc. and
all by the age of 22!

I wasn't lucky enough to choose a career, as I have always been unemployable, but jewellery chose me in a series of strange and kismet-like ways. It ended up being the only one of a series of creative endeavours that I could make a living out of – failed poet, songwriter, musician, writer, portrait-painter, etc. and all by the age of 22!

THEO FENNELL

THEO FENNELL

A sensitive and meticulous person, with a clear sense of his goals, he is coolly detached and self-contained which enhances his objectivity. He is organised in his affairs, prudent and cautious. He is a perfectionist with a refined and delicate sense of aestheticism. He has original sense of style and a personal way of looking at things.

As he does not like to divulge his feelings, he is an enigma and not easy to get to know. He protects himself through immersion in work, which he approaches with quiet reflection and a high degree of concentration. He is selective in his choice of friends, and on an intimate level, he will show warmth of feeling and gentleness.

In all, an unusual and unique person, discretely determined to achieve in his own way.

16

BRYAN FORBES

Film Director & Author

New Sights

I like to see a thing I know
Has not been seen before,
That's why I cut my apple through
To look into the core.

It's nice to think, though many an eye
Has seen the ruddy skin,
Mine's the very first to spy
The five brown pips within.

        — Anon.

NEW SIGHTS

I like to see a thing I know
Has not been seen before,
That's why I cut my apple through
To look into the core.

It's nice to think, though many an eye
Has seen the ruddy skin,
Mine is the very first to spy
The five brown pips within.

Anon.

When I was very small I went on
holiday to a farm and it was the
first time I had ever been exposed
to animals ~ horses, cows, pigs, chickens ~
for I lived in a town. I was allowed
to go and search for eggs in the hedgerows
where the free-range chickens made their
nests, and I remember the thrill of suddenly
coming upon eggs that were still warm.
It was like discovering gold coins.

When I was very small I went on holiday to a farm and it was the first time I had ever been exposed to animals – horses, cows, pigs, chickens – for I lived in a town. I was allowed to go and search for eggs in the hedgerows where the free-range chickens made their nests, and I remember the thrill of suddenly coming upon eggs that were still warm. It was like discovering gold coins.

BRYAN FORBES

The writer is a careful, thorough and down-to-earth person. Self-absorbed, it is difficult to distract him from his aims, as he is tenacious and single-minded.

He analyses and weighs up situations before embarking on an outcome. Concern for presentation, deliberation and a sense of his own worth impart a craftsman's attitude to what he does.

On the intellectual level, he concentrates well, is efficient and assimilates selective information.

His dedication to the task in hand makes it difficult for others to change his mind. He prefers to keep relationships within a professional framework and getting close to him is not easy.

His successful career is due to his persistency and determination.

17

EMMA FORBES

Television Presenter

Peter Piper

Peter Piper picked a peck of pickled peppers.

A peck of pickled peppers Peter Piper picked.

If Peter Piper picked a peck of pickled peppers,

Where's the peck of pickled peppers Peter Pipe picked?

PETER PIPER

Peter Piper picked a peck of pickled peppers;
A peck of pickled peppers Peter Piper picked.
If Peter Piper picked a peck of pickled peppers,
Where's the peck of pickled peppers Peter Piper
  picked?

Traditional

I chose TV presenting as a career, because I think it is such an exciting industry to be part of, forever changing + new challenges all the time - I feel very lucky to love what I do.

I chose TV presenting as a career, because I think it is such an exciting industry to be part of, forever changing and new challenges all the time – I feel very lucky to love what I do.

EMMA FORBES

As the writer is practical, she is more interested in down-to-earth and social matters rather than in abstract concepts.

She can be charming, set in her views and is able to preserve some distance out of caution and secretiveness as she has a strong sense of self-protection and does not take risks. She is able to exert considerable control on her emotions and environment and therefore she is careful and deliberates before she acts.

She is persistent, thorough and well organised in whatever she undertakes to do. She appears confident and adapts to circumstances with apparent ease, making the most of her opportunities at times with a fist of iron in a velvet glove if needs be. She asserts herself strongly and can command respect and attention.

18

ANNA FORD

Broadcaster & Journalist

Brother.

I had a little brother
And I brought him to my mother
And I said I want another
Little brother for a change.
But she said don't be a bother
So I took him to my father
And I said this little bother
Of a brother's very strange.

But he said one little brother
Is exactly like another
And every little brother
Misbehaves a bit he said.
So I took the little brother
From my mother & my father
And I put the little brother
Of a brother back to bed.

MARY ANN HOBERMAN.

BROTHER

I had a little brother
And I brought him to my mother
And I said I want another
Little brother for a change.
But she said don't be a bother
So I took him to my father
And I said this little bother
Of a brother's very strange.

But he said one little brother
Is exactly like another
And every little brother
Misbehaves a bit he said.
So I took the little bother
From my mother and my father
And I put the little bother
Of a brother back to bed.

Mary Ann Hoberman

Climbing over a hot, slate
style into a hayfield, full
of wild flowers. Poppies,
harebells bladder campion
burnet, mayflower, scabious.
A tiny stream ran under
some flat slates making
a bridge, down to a big
pool ("the dub") in the river.
There was a beach of
round grey pebbles, very
clean & the water was very
cold & dark green.
We often had a picnic here
& swam in the freezing
water which took your
breath away.

Anna Ford.

Climbing over a hot, slate stile into a hayfield, full of wild flowers. Poppies, harebells, bladder campion, burnet, mayflower, scabions. A tiny stream ran under some flat slates making a bridge, down to a big pool ('The dub') in the river. There was a beach of round grey pebbles, very clean and the water was very cold and dark green. We often had a picnic here and swam in the freezing water which took your breath away.

ANNA FORD

Broad in her outlook she has an animated mind, and her interest would lie more in the every day world of human affairs than with esoteric theory or narrow specialisation.

She has a spontaneous sociability and an intuitive understanding of the world about her.

Inclined sometimes towards impulsivity, she could become impatient with mechanical routine or dull mediocrity, as she has a vivid imagination and sets herself high standards. However, caution touched with discipline is usually able to override any volatility and channel her energies productively. Sensitive, she is subject to anxieties and will be quick to react.

In contention she would stand her ground with tenacity, but she has a generosity of spirit and she would not harbour grudges.

19

HUGH GRANT

Actor

Who has seen the wind?
Neither you nor I:
But when the trees bow down their heads
The wind is passing by.

— Christina Rossetti.

WHO HAS SEEN THE WIND?

Who has seen the wind?
Neither you nor I:
But when the trees bow down their heads
The wind is passing by.

Christina Rossetti

One of the moments I remember most
vividly from childhood was – when
I was about four – deciding it
would be interesting to stuff some
apple peel up my nose. I made
a very good job of it and London's
most senior ear, nose and throat
doctor spent several hours removing
it.

— Hugh Grant.

One of the moments I remember most vividly from childhood was – when I was about four – deciding it would be interesting to stuff some apple peel up my nose. I made a very good job of it and London's most senior ear, nose and throat doctor spent several hours removing it.

HUGH GRANT

The writer has an agile intelligence, sophistication and thoughtful intuitive mind.

Open to new ideas, he is able to perceive possibilities and yet distance himself sufficiently to remain objective and independent.

He is tolerant of others, modest and realistic towards himself; this, together with an apparent ease of communication, plus a humour, ensures a certain degree of social adaptability. However there is a more serious underlying aspect to his personality.

Whilst there is an aesthetic concern for presentation, order and precision in the short term, he remains wary of bold long term decisions, preferring if possible to keep future options open.

Instinctively he is able to exploit his talents productively without undue waste of energy – for example in an aggressive pursuit of fame just for its own sake. His successes would appear to be achieved without much effort.

20

RICHARD E. GRANT

Actor

'There was an old man!'
There was on old man
          with a beard.
Who said, 'It's just as I feared
Two owls and a hen
four larks and a wren
Have all built their nests
    in my beard!'

Edward Lear (1812-188

'THERE WAS AN OLD MAN...'

There was an Old Man with a beard,
Who said, 'It is just as I feared! –
Two Owls and a Hen,
four Larks and a Wren,
Have all built their nests in my beard!'

Edward Lear

I always wanted to be an
actor/writer and have never
wavered from that wish.
I'm very grateful that all
those people who predicted
otherwise have been proved wrong.

Richard E. Grant.

I always wanted to be an actor/writer and have never wavered from that wish. I'm very grateful that all those people who predicted otherwise, have been proved wrong.

RICHARD E. GRANT

This is a man of broadly based intelligence, someone who takes a wide view of life. He is resourceful in commanding attention. A certain flamboyance and flair enable him to inspire and motivate others.

With strong imagination and natural extraversion, he has the ability to embellish in a captivating manner.

Versatile and labile, he needs to be kept occupied. He is impatient for immediate results. Having some inner uncertainties, he keeps himself busy and finds stimulation in the way he can assume a variety of roles.

21

SUSAN HAMPSHIRE

Actress

Chocolates.

Here are the seats, George, old man,
Get some chocolates while you can.

Quick the curtain's going to rise,
(Either Cadburys or Spry's)

"The Castle Ramparts Elsinore
(That's Not sufficient, get some more)

There's the 'Ghost', he does look wan
(Help yourself, and pass them on)

Doesn't 'Hamlet' do it well?
(This one is a caramel)

'Polonius's' beard is fine
(Don't you grab; that big one's mine)

Look the 'King' can't bear the play
(Throw that squashy one away)

Now the 'King' is at his prayers
(Splendid there are two more layers)

'Hamlet' going for his mother
(Come on, Tony, have another)

Poor 'Ophelia'! Look, she's mad
(However many's Betty's had?)

The 'Queen' is dead and so's the King
(Keep that lovely silver string)

Now even 'Hamlet' can no more
(Pig! You've dropped it on the floor)

The last Act's simply full of shocks
(There's several left, so bring the box)

Guy Boas Punch 1925

CHOCOLATES

Here the seats are; George, old man,
Get some chocolates while you can.
Quick, the curtain's going to rise
(Either Bradbury's or Spry's).
'The Castle ramparts, Elsinore'
(That's not sufficient, get some more).
There's the *Ghost*: he does look wan
Help yourself and pass them on.
Doesn't *Hamlet* do it well?
(This one's a caramel).
Polonius's beard is fine
(Don't you grab; that big one's mine).
Look, the *King* can't hear the play
(Throw that squashy one away).
Now the *King* is at his prayers
(Splendid! there are two more layers).
Hamlet's going for his mother
(Come on, Tony, have another).
Poor *Ophelia*! Look she's mad
(However many's Betty had?).
The *Queen* is dead and so's the *King*
(Keep that lovely silver string).
Now even *Hamlet* can no more
(Pig! You've dropped it on the floor).
That last Act's simply full of shocks
(There's several left, so bring the box).

Guy Boas

123

CHILD HOOD MEMORY

A childhood memory, that is hard
not just because I'm finding it more
and more difficult to remember my childhood
but because I find writing a piece of this
sort makes me feel that I am in some way
being tested or judged — which I know,
given my profession is silly of me — since
I spend my whole life being judged!

My Mother had a fur coat, and when she
wore it it had a lovely smell, her warm
body, the fur & the coat. As a child I used
to walk behind my Mother under the
coat my arms round her waist and my
head resting on her back — So warm & snug
like a back to front Kangaroo.

I loved the smell

Susan Hampshire

Childhood Memory

A childhood memory, that is hard not just because I'm finding it more and more difficult to remember my childhood but because I find writing a piece of this sort makes me feel that I am in some way being tested and judged – which I know, given my profession is silly of me – since I spend my whole life being judged!

My mother had a fur coat, and when she wore it it had a lovely smell. I loved the smell of her warm body, the fur and the coat. As a child I used to walk behind my Mother under the coat my arms round her waist and my head resting on her back – so warm and snug like a back to front kangaroo.

SUSAN HAMPSHIRE

Optimistic, creative, adaptable and spontaneous, the writer has a strong need to achieve.

She is adept at seeing opportunities and improvising solutions. Logical and perceptive she sees things in practical terms. Her intuitive understanding enables her to put herself in other people's shoes. She can be diplomatic but will not shrink from speaking her mind when necessary.

A lively and easy communicator she is candid about herself and could enjoy a public role with ease and grace.

There is a nervous intensity, which keeps her in a state of habitual expectancy. Generosity of spirit and warmth of personality give her a natural charm.

22

NICK HORNBY

Writer

WISHES OF AN ELDERLY MAN

I wish I loved the Human Race
I wish I loved its silly face;
I wish I liked the way it walks
I wish I liked the way it talks;
And when I'm introduced to one
I wish I thought 'What Jolly Fun'!

WISHES OF AN ELDERLY MAN

I wish I loved the Human Race;
I wish I loved its silly face;
I wish I liked the way it walks;
I wish I liked the way it talks;
And when I'm introduced to one
I wish I thought *What Jolly Fun!*

Sir Walter Raleigh

I became a writer because I hate having to get up in the morning, get on the tube and go to an office in a suit. I became a writer because it's one of the only things I can do with any competence. And I became a writer because I have a need to write.

Nick Hornby

I became a writer because I hate having to get up in the morning, get on the tube and go to an office in a suit. I became a writer because it's one of the only things I can do with any competence. And I became a writer because I have a need to write.

NICK HORNBY

The writer has a sharp, clever, agile and critical mind. His thinking is factual, perceptive and astute, versatile and cohesive. He can analyse and synthesise, as well as view situations globally.

Influenced by his emotions, he can be somewhat stubborn and consequently defensive at times, but whatever he feels strongly about actually helps motivate him into action, and provides an outlet into the creative activity that his fertile mind is capable of. He needs to express and assert himself.

He is energetic and needs physical as well as mental activity. He is thorough in his undertakings, but would find routine tasks unbearable.

He is able to spot an absurdity quickly and he will be amused by it rather than dismiss it.

23

SHIRLEY HUGHES

Author & Illustrator

GIRL FRIENDS
Shirley Hughes

Marian, Lily and Annie Rose
Are three bonny girls, as everyone knows.
Sometimes bouncy, sometimes sad,
Sometimes sleepy, sometimes glad,
Sometimes grubby, sometimes clean,
Often kind, though sometimes mean.
But most of the time they try to be good,
And to all that know them it's understood
That Marian, Lily and Annie Rose
Are best of friends, as everyone knows.

from 'RHYMES for ANNIE ROSE'

GIRL FRIENDS

Marian, Lily and Annie Rose
Are three bonny girls, as everyone knows.
Sometimes bouncy, sometimes sad,
Sometimes sleepy, sometimes glad,
Sometimes grubby, sometimes clean
Often kind, though sometimes mean.
But most of the time they try to be good,
And to all that know them it's understood
That Marian, Lily and Annie Rose
Are best of friends, as everyone knows.

Shirley Hughes

When I was a child in World War II we
lived in a so-called 'safe' area near
Liverpool. I carried a gasmask to
school and did air-raid drill and slept
under the stairs during the winter
of the big blitz. But the trouble with
that time was that when it wasn't
frightening it was very boring. We
couldn't go on holiday, there was
never anything nice to eat and the
grownups were too exhausted and anxious
to entertain us.

We read a lot, and drew and got
up plays and acted them to whoever
would watch. With me, drawing stuck.
I just went on doing it. I liked writing
too, but it was a secret thing which
I kept under wraps. I expect I became
an illustrator and writer because
the only really exciting thing at
that time was inventing stories.

Shirley Hughes

When I was a child in World War II we lived in a so-called 'safe' area near Liverpool. I carried a gasmask to school and did air-raid drill and slept under the stairs during the winter of the big blitz. But the trouble with that time was that when it wasn't frightening it was very boring. We couldn't go on holiday, there was never anything nice to eat and the grownups were too exhausted and anxious to entertain us.

We read a lot, and drew and got up plays and acted them to whoever would watch. With me, drawing stuck. I just went on doing it. I liked writing too, but it was a secret thing which I kept under wraps. I expect I became an illustrator and writer because the only really exciting thing at that time was inventing stories.

SHIRLEY HUGHES

SHIRLEY HUGHES

Self-motivated with vitality and stamina, she has inner strength and approaches life with confidence. Her self-discipline and principled sense of duty do not preclude a tolerant understanding of others.

Perceptively observant, she relates well to her immediate surroundings. She will be kind, helpful and understanding in an objective way.

Her creative and sensitive mind enables her to present daily events with an aesthetic lyricism.

24

JEREMY IRONS

Actor

Tweedle-dum and Tweedle-dee
Resolved to have a battle.
For Tweedle-dum said Tweedle-dee
Had spoiled his nice new rattle.

Just then flew by a monstrous crow
As big as a tar-barrel,
Which frightened both the heroes so
They quite forgot their quarrel.

TWEEDLE-DUM AND TWEEDLE-DEE

Tweedle-dum and Tweedle-dee
Resolved to have a battle
For Tweedle-dum said Tweedle-dee
Had spoiled his nice new rattle.

Just then flew by a monstrous crow
As big as a tar-barrel,
Which frightened both the heroes so
They quite forgot their quarrel.

Lewis Carroll

I remember the first time I was placed
on the back of a horse. It was in a stable
and the horse was grey.
I remember it seeming quite nice, but rather high.

Jeremy Thomas.

I remember the first time I was placed on the back of a horse. It was in a stable and the horse was grey.
I remember it seeming quite nice, but rather high.

JEREMY IRONS

This is a supple, cultured, sensitive mind, coolly under control. The result is a harmonious co-ordination of ideas and actions. The writer's breadth of outlook and spirit of enquiry is steadied by a certain detached objectivity.

His discriminating mind grasps essentials, senses possibilities and creatively develops ideas without losing sight of details. He can thus achieve his goals without undue waste of energy.

Though self-affirming and independent-minded, he nonetheless works well with others and inspires confidence by virtue of subtlety and disciplined high standards, not noisy self-assertion, which he would regard as in questionable taste.

Socially he is adaptable and diplomatic with a perceptive understanding of others. He is perhaps less easy revealing his own personal emotions, so that in some sense it is through his profession that he more freely expresses himself.

25

CLIVE KING

Writer

Stopping by woods on a Snowy Evening

Whose woods these are I think I know.
His house is in the village, though;
He will not see me stopping here
To watch his woods fill up with snow.

My little horse must think it queer
To stop without a farmhouse near
Between the woods and frozen lake
The darkest evening of the year.

He gives his harness bells a shake
To ask if there is some mistake.
The only other sound's the sweep
Of easy wind and downy flake.

The woods are lovely, dark, and deep
But I have promises to keep
And miles to go before I sleep,
And miles to go before I sleep.

                    Robert Frost (1874 - 1963)

STOPPING BY WOODS ON A SNOWY EVENING

Whose woods these are I think I know.
His house is in the village, though;
He will not see me stopping here
To watch his woods fill up with snow.

My little horse must think it queer
To stop without a farmhouse near
Between the woods and frozen lake
The darkest evening of the year.

He gives his harness bells a shake
To ask if there is some mistake
The only other sound's the sweep
Of easy wind and downy flake.

The woods are lovely, dark, and deep,
But I have promises to keep,
And miles to go before I sleep,
And miles to go before I sleep.

Robert Frost

It was the first winter of World War Two,
and the beginning of 1940 was very
cold and snowy. Our boarding school
had left the city and taken refuge
in the old Abbey at Bayham, deep in
the Kentish countryside. We used to
dare each other to go down alone from our
freezing dormitory into the ancient ruins
and pull the rope of the bell that hung
there. Up to then I was afraid of the
dark, but I went and pulled the bell and —
nothing happened. No story! But I was
cured of my night fears. When the snows
melted the floods came and I witnessed
a raft of debris carrying a helpless
little animal towards the waterfall. Nothing
I could do to help — and, anyway, worse
things were happening to our sailors at sea.
But yes, it inspired me to write my
first children's story, with my own illustrations.
I wasn't sure whether I wanted to be
a writer or an artist, but war was
the priority and I was called up for
the navy.

Clive King

It was the first winter of World War Two, and the beginning of 1940 was very cold and snowy. Our boarding school had left the city and taken refuge in The Old Abbey at Bayham, deep in the Kentish countryside. We used to dare each other to go down alone from our freezing dormitory into the ancient ruins and pull the rope of the bell that hung there. Up to then I was afraid of the dark, but I went and pulled the bell and – nothing happened. No story! But I was cured of my night fears. When the snows melted the floods came and I witnessed a raft of debris carrying a helpless little animal towards the waterfall. Nothing I could do to help – and, anyway, worse things were happening to our sailors at sea. But yes, it inspired me to write my first children's story, with my own illustrations. I wasn't sure whether I wanted to be a writer or an artist, but war was the priority and I was called up for the navy.

CLIVE KING

This aesthetically sensitive man is both astute and receptive. He has acuteness of vision, keen perception and a clear and lucid mind.

Intuitive and curious, his judgements are based on fact and his thinking is logical and objective.

He is very persistent and a strict traditionalist who is demanding of himself.

He has a decided sense of purpose, is mature in his approach to life, albeit with a subtle sense of humour coloured by poetical tendencies.

His profession fulfils his need for self-expression, which gives him a sense of satisfaction.

26

FRANK LEBOEUF

Professional Football Player

The park.

I'm glad that I live near a park
For in the winter after dark
The park lights shine as bright and still
As dandelions on a hill

James S. TIPPETT

THE PARK

I'm glad that I
Live near a park

For in the winter
After dark

The park lights shine
As bright and still

As dandelions
On a hill.

James S. Tippett

Why I chose my particular career?

First of all, could you please forgive me for my miserable english. I'm going to do my best but some grammatical or spelling or even syntax mistakes might be found.

Football is my life, I've always played that game when I was young and I even think I was born with a football.

My father has been a football player, my manager afterward, and he taught me all basics you need to be a pretty good player. I didn't really have to choose my future, it was my destiny and Thanks god for having shown me the way of success.

F. LEBOEUF

Why I chose my particular career?

First of all, could you please forgive me for my miserable English. I'm going to do my best but some grammatical or spelling or even syntax mistakes might be found.

Football is my life, I've always played that game when I was young and I even think I was born with a football.

My father has been a football player, my manager afterward, and he taught me all basics you need to be a pretty good player. I didn't really have to choose my future, it was my destiny and Thanks god for having shown me the way of success.

F. LEBOEUF

FRANK LEBOEUF

Boyish in his outlook with energy and a need for activity, this man has a sense of order and self-control. He has strong determination, persistence, courage and dynamism. Clear in his aims, he needs to feel part of a structured environment with well defined ground rules, in order to be at his best. Hence he operates well in a team whilst also using his own initiative.

On the whole self-disciplined, he is also down-to-earth, sensible, practical and thinks before acting.

With people, he is friendly, co-operative and sociable, but likes to keep a certain aspect of his character to himself.

He has a well balanced, careful and stable personality, and is conscientious, reliable and has the ambition to do well in what he does.

27

CHRISTOPHER LEE

Actor, Singer & Author

There was a little rabbit
who was laying in his burrow,
when the Dingo rang him up to say
he'd call on him tomorrow.

But the rabbit thought it better
that the Dingo did'nt meet him.
So he found another burrow
and the Dingo did'nt eat him.

Christopher Lee

THE CLEVER RABBIT

There was a little rabbit
who was lying in his burrow,
when the Dingo rang him up to say
he'd call on him tomorrow.

But the rabbit thought it better
that the Dingo didn't meet him.
So he found another burrow
and the Dingo didn't eat him.

D. H. Souter

I have so many childhood memories that is difficult to pick just one.

But I think the incident that most affected me, at the age of about twelve or thirteen was when I took part in a Fox Hunt with the West Somerset Foxhounds and was "blooded" on each cheek with the blood of the fox, after the kill.

I was similarly present at the "gralloch" and death of a stag with the Devon and Somerset Staghounds, at the same age.

I was so appalled by these two incidents that I swore I would never hunt animals again. And I never have. I gave up rough shooting in 1948.

Christopher Lee

I have so many childhood memories that is difficult to pick just one.

But I think the incident that most affected me, at the age of about twelve or thirteen was when I took part in a fox hunt with the West Somerset Foxhounds and was 'blooded' on each cheek with the blood of the fox, after the kill.

I was similarly present at the 'gralloch' and death of a stag with the Devon and Somerset Staghounds, at the same age.

I was so appalled by these two incidents that I swore I would never hunt animals again. And I never have. I gave up rough shooting in 1948.

CHRISTOPHER LEE

CHRISTOPHER LEE

The writer is a cultured man who sets himself high standards and has the initiative, discipline and thoroughness to achieve his goals. His general outlook is intellectual and realistic rather than emotional and temperamental. His thinking is therefore logical, clear and flexible and any show of emotion is kept under control. He has a subtlety of perception, independence and powers of concentration, which together make for creative associative processes.

He keeps active and displays finesse and aestheticism in what he does.

He is a man of conviction and high ethical principles which he will not compromise. There is a certain reserve in expressing more intimate feelings, thus protecting underlying sensitivities. These however are a source of enrichment in terms of insight and understanding and are also a stimulus for outgoing attitudes and undertakings.

Although sociable and communicative, he is selective in his choice of friends and exercises cautious receptivity.

An impressive, distinguished, autonomous personality, he is a man of integrity who can command authority by virtue of his ability and example.

28

DAVID LODGE

Writer

Weeping Willow in My Garden

My willow's like a frozen hill
Of green waves, when the wind is still;
But when it blows, the waves unfreeze
And make a waterfall of leaves.

IAN SERRAILLIER

WEEPING WILLOW IN MY GARDEN

My willow's like a frozen hill
Of green waves, when the wind is still;
But when it blows, the waves unfreeze
And make a waterfall of leaves.

Ian Serraillier

When I was very young, perhaps three or four, I was in my garden in London and an adult pointed at the sky and said "Look, David, there's an airship." I had never seen an airship, or a picture of one, so what I was looking for was a ship, with funnels and smoke, like the Queen Mary, sailing across the sky. And I was sure I saw one, very high up and far away. I looked for airships many times after that, but to my disappointment I never saw another one.

David Lodge

20/5/99

When I was very young, perhaps three or four, I was in my garden in London and an adult pointed at the sky and said "Look, David, there's an airship." I had never seen an airship, or a picture of one, so what I was looking for was a ship, with funnels and smoke, like the *Queen Mary*, sailing across the sky. And I was sure I saw one, very high up and far away. I looked for airships many times after that, but to my disappointment I never saw another one.

DAVID LODGE

The man's energy is largely devoted to intellectual rather than material pursuits. He has imagination and is free from conventional thinking. He is intuitive, curious, subtle, very alert and agile in his thinking. He is sensitive to outside nuances and uses his insight to fulfil his creative aspirations.

His vibrant emotions stimulate him into productive creativity, rather than getting too involved personally with people. He enjoys communication and is sociable, but has little time for small talk.

He is understanding, tolerant and unpedantic towards others, and has a witty sense of irony about life.

29

FELICITY LOTT

Singer

Two Men Looked Out.

Two men looked out through prison bars;
The one saw mud, the other stars.

TWO MEN LOOKED OUT

Two men looked out through prison bars;
The one saw mud, the other stars.

Anon.

I think my career chose me: singing was — and still is — what I most enjoy doing. I can't believe that I've managed to make it last so long, without someone telling me to wake up and get a proper job!

I think my career chose me: singing was – and still is – what I most enjoy doing. I can't believe that I've managed to make it last so long, without someone telling me to wake up and get a proper job!

FELICITY LOTT

FELICITY LOTT

This is an outgoing person with self-confidence grounded in discipline and order.

Her judgement is objective and her notions well directed, so that, in achieving her goals, she can keep to essentials without fuss or waste of energy.

She has imagination, flair, and performing quality, but her balanced sense of proportion and critical faculty are always in control.

Her social warmth and adaptability would enable her to work well and express her creativity without compromising her integrity.

30

JOANNA LUMLEY

Actress

'Twinkle, twinkle, little bat'

Twinkle, Twinkle, little bat!
How I wonder what you're at!
Up above the world you fly,
Like a tea-tray in the sky.

Lewis Carroll (1832 - 1898)

'TWINKLE, TWINKLE, LITTLE BAT'

Twinkle, twinkle, little bat!
How I wonder what you're at!
Up above the world you fly,
Like a tea-tray in the sky.

Lewis Carroll

When I was three years old and
living in Hong Kong I made up my
first poem. It was:
The cat sat on the road
Suddenly came a car
And runned it over.
Up jumped the bandage
And the plaster
And popped it on.
Even then I knew I lacked
   Something.

Joanna Lumley

When I was three years old and living in Hong Kong
I made up my first poem. It was:

The cat sat on the road
Suddenly came a car
And runned it over.
Up jumped the bandage
And the plaster
And popped it on.

Even then I knew I lacked something.

JOANNA LUMLEY

JOANNA LUMLEY

This is a self-motivated person with a supple and independent judgement. Outgoing and with social charm, she still remains sufficiently detached to preserve her own privacy and autonomy.

Straightforward and self-reliant, she stands her ground in situations of contention. While she is self-disciplined and conscientious, there is an underlying impatience with routine, whereas she finds change stimulating.

Astute and realistic, she has instinctive under-standing of herself and others. An impressive personality, she carries herself with dignity and pride.

31

SIR ROGER MOORE

Actor

Little Jack Horner
Sat in a corner,
Eating his Christmas pie;
He put in his thumb,
And pulled out a plum,
And said, "What a good boy am I!"

LITTLE JACK HORNER

Little Jack Horner
Sat in a corner,
Eating his Christmas pie;
He put in his thumb,
And pulled out a plum,
And said, 'What a good boy am I!'

Traditional

My 'career' as such is on what you might call the 'backburner' — reason being I now and have been for the past nine years a representative of UNICEF — The United Nations Children's Fund.

Much more important than 'acting'! I do not intend that to sound pompous — it is the plain truth —

I have seen many of the children in the camps & schools in Macedonia. They desperately need to return to their homes — God willing it will be soon.

[signature]
3rd June 1999

My 'career' as such is on what you might call the 'backburner' – reason being I now and have been for the last nine years a representative of UNICEF – The United Nations Children's Fund.

Much more important than 'acting'! I do not intend that to sound pompous – it is the plain truth –

I have seen many of the children in the camps and schools in Macedonia. They desperately need to return to their homes – God willing it will be soon.

ROGER MOORE

He is an organised and sensitive person who marshals his time and resources in an orderly and disciplined fashion.

The quality of presentation is important to him. He takes personal pride in achieving high standards in whatever he undertakes.

He is stable, thorough and conscientious in his approach. He is courteous and diplomatic but will stand his ground when needed.

A clear, logical and sharp mind, capable of reflective thought, he is self-reliant, and disinclined to rely on others.

32

SIR ROGER NORRINGTON

Conductor

A Change in the Year

It is the first mild day of March:
Each minute sweeter than before,
The red-breast sings from the tall larch
That stands beside our door.

There is a blessing in the air,
Which seems a sense of joy to yield
To the bare trees, and mountains bare;
And grass in the green field.

William Wordsworth

A CHANGE IN THE YEAR

It is the first mild day of March:
Each minute sweeter than before,
The red-breast sings from the tall larch
That stands beside our door.

There is a blessing in the air,
Which seems a sense of joy to yield
To the bare trees, and mountains bare;
And grass in the green field.

William Wordsworth

What a memorable moment it was for
me when, at the age of ten, I first saw
New York City, with the skyscrapers mostly
just built. It was the only place in the
world you could see such enormous
buildings at that time. I basked in
the amazement of it all, and then left
for England, on an aircraft carrier.

Roger Norrington

What a memorable moment it was for me when, at the age of ten, I first saw New York City, with the skyscrapers mostly just built. It was the only place in the world you could see such enormous buildings at that time. I basked in the amazement of it all, and then left for England, on an aircraft carrier.

ROGER NORRINGTON

SIR ROGER NORRINGTON

This is a man with clarity of mind, a perceptive sensitivity and tenacity. He is a perfectionist in his work, organised, disciplined, meticulous over details and demanding both of himself and others.

His emotions are strong and long lasting and he responds quickly, though not impulsively, to impressions that affect him. He takes pride in striving to do well. Not a vain man, he nonetheless has a sense of his own worth, and commands respect accordingly.

He is an idealist whose feelings run deep, but his analytical, logical mind, ability to concentrate and his concern for high standards enable him to override any inner sensibilities which might otherwise hamper his creativity.

He has a curiosity of mind and a forward-looking attitude, yet, on balance, it is his inner challenges rather than more superficial outside imperatives that provide his driving force.

This unusual combination of character features has led to his success.

33

TONY O'REILLY

Company Director

Think where mans glory.
Most begins and ends.
- And say "My glory was.
I had such friends'

                    William Butler Yeats

THE MUNICIPAL GALLERY REVISITED (EXTRACT)

Think where man's glory most begins and ends,
And say my glory was I had such friends.

W. B. Yeats

My Childhood was made very
special by the constant presence
of a Magician — My Mother!

As an only child I was with
her all the time — she was my
perfect window on the world

And never again wants the lens
of life be so clear.

My childhood was made very special by the constant presence of a magician – my mother!

As an only child I was with her all the time – she was my perfect window on the world and never again would the lens of life be so clear.

TONY O'REILLY

This writer has a supple, adaptable mind with a rapid grasp of situations and an aptitude for seizing the right opportunities as they present themselves.

His judgements are clear, incorporating as they do deductive, emotional and intuitive elements in appropriate measure.

Socially he is confident and cordial and likes to feel at the centre of what is going on. Nevertheless there is an underlying vigilance prompting a certain detachment.

He can adapt to a variety of social environments through his keen intelligence, imparting a critical – even caustic – wit. His humour, inventive imagination and verbal agility make him stimulating company for others.

There is an aesthetic appreciation and an easy sense of style and presentation in the way he conducts himself and his affairs.

34

BRUCE OLDFIELD

Fashion Designer

Row, Row, Row the boat

Row, row, row the boat
Gently down the stream,
Merrily, merrily merrily,
                merrily
Life is but a dream.

ROW, ROW, ROW THE BOAT

Row, row, row the boat
Gently down the stream,
Merrily, merrily, merrily, merrily,
Life is but a dream.

Traditional

A memorable moment for me at school was when I performed in the school play (albeit very briefly) without stammering — a nerve-wracking yet satisfying experience.

I chose my career as it seemed to be the best way to channel what I liked doing into what could give me some financial stability. We seemed suited!

A memorable moment for me at school was when I performed in the school play (albeit very briefly) without stammering – a nerve-wracking yet satisfying experience.

I chose my career as it seemed to be the best way to channel what I liked doing into what could give me some financial stability. We seemed suited!

BRUCE OLDFIELD

BRUCE OLDFIELD

Enthusiasm, imagination and creativity are ingredients in this dynamic and decisive personality. Enterprising and impatient to achieve his goals, he immerses himself immediately in his projects.

He often relies on his ability to improvise rather than preparing in advance, preferring to delegate plodding details to somebody else.

He is a very talented marketing man, who is sociable and adaptable on his own terms. He understands immediately where his interests lie, and communicates well accordingly.

He is dynamic and decisive with a flexible and agile mind. His thinking is quick and he prefers mistakes made due to rapid decisions rather than mistakes made due to slow decisions.

He is a charismatic man with a sense of style.

35

JOHN S. PARKER

Director of Cambridge University Botanic Garden

A Baby Sardine

A baby sardine
Saw her first submarine
She was scared and watched through a peephole

"Oh come, come, come,"
Said the sardine's mum.
"It's only a tin full of people."

A BABY SARDINE

A baby sardine
Saw her first submarine:
She was scared and watched through a peephole.

'Oh come, come, come,'
Said the sardine's mum.
'It's only a tin full of people.'

Spike Milligan

I became fascinated by flowers one day
aged 10 when my eyes were opened
by a sudden realisation of how beautiful
they were. I was on holiday with my
parents in North Wales when the sheer
exuberance of species struck me. I loved
them immediately and have been a botanist
ever since

I became fascinated by flowers one day aged 10 when my eyes were opened by a sudden realisation of how beautiful they were. I was on holiday with my parents in North Wales when the sheer exuberance of species struck me. I loved them immediately and have been a botanist ever since.

J. S. PARKER

JOHN S. PARKER

This is a clearly defined personality, methodical, systematic and self-sufficient. He is practical and creative with a strong professional attitude. There is concern for proper order and classification. He appreciates the world of the senses and is responsive to colour, form and texture. At work he is firm in his decisions and able to command authority.

Rather a perfectionist, he is more concerned with quality rather than quantity. There is warmth of personality especially for those close to him, yet nonetheless he can be somewhat detached, which allows him to pursue his own interests and passions.

36

PHILIPPA PEARCE

Children's Author

A Cradle Song

Golden slumbers kiss your eyes,
Smiles await you when you rise,
Sleep pretty wantons, do not cry,
And I will sing a lullaby:
Rock them, rock them, lullaby.

Care is heavy, therefore sleep you;
You are care, and care must keep you,
Sleep, pretty wantons, do not cry,
And I will sing a lullaby;
Rock them, rock them, lullaby.

Thomas Dekker (1572-1632)

A CRADLE SONG

Golden slumbers kiss your eyes,
Smiles awake you when you rise.
Sleep, pretty wantons, do not cry,
And I will sing a lullaby:
Rock them, rock them, lullaby.

Care is heavy, therefore sleep you;
You are care, and care must keep you.
Sleep, pretty wantons, do not cry,
And I will sing a lullaby:
Rock them, rock them, lullaby.

Thomas Dekker (1572–1632)

I think that a memorable moment
must have been my first ice cream —
a strawberry cone which eventually
dripped from my palm to the point of
my elbow.

Philippa Pearce

I <u>think</u> that memorable moment must have been my first ice cream – a strawberry cone which eventually dripped from my palm to the point of my elbow.

PHILIPPA PEARCE

PHILIPPA PEARCE

A genuine and sensitive person, who is persistent in her endeavours. She has an inquisitive mind with deductive thinking and powers of concentration.

She is modest about herself, broad-minded in her views, diplomatic, patient and tolerant. In spite of her age, she is youthful in her outlook and this may be the key to her choice of profession, since it helps her more easily to identify with young minds.

37

SIR CHARLES POWELL

Businessman

A Frog and a Flea

A frog and a flea
And a kangaroo
Once jumped for a prize
In a pot of glue.
The kangaroo stuck
And so did the flea,
And the frog limped home
With a fractured knee

Cynthia Mitchell

A FROG AND A FLEA

A frog and a flea
And a kangaroo
Once jumped for a prize
In a pot of glue;
The kangaroo stuck
And so did the flea,
And the frog limped home
With a fractured knee.

Cynthia Mitchell

Singing my first evensong
as a cathedral chorister
in Canterbury Cathedral, amid
the towering Gothic magnificence
and gloom, and hearing the
voices carried upwards e
away as others had been
over the centuries, and
experiencing a sense of
history for the first time
in my short life.

Charles Powell

Singing my first evensong as a cathedral chorister in Canterbury Cathedral, amid the towering Gothic magnificence and gloom, and hearing the voices carried upwards and away as others had been over the centuries, and experiencing a sense of history for the first time in my short life.

CHARLES POWELL

This is a self-motivated man, ambitious, spirited and independent minded. He retains, from his past and upbringing, a sense of order and method, which helps to channel his energies productively towards achievement of goals.

An intuitive resourcefulness and ability to appraise situations from an objective distance facilitates clarity of initiative and quick decisions.

Socially he has charm, diplomacy and generosity. Such general cordiality is in some measure countered by an underlying defensiveness or even a potential for revolt, should he feel he was being unduly put upon, or taken for granted.

Possessed of a discerning aesthetic sense, he enjoys the good things of life and likes to spread himself. He is self-confident and takes a broad outlook. Within his field of operation he is naturally authoritative and this can be useful in inspiring others and getting things done.

38

PHILIP PULLMAN

Author

Ariel's Song

Full fathom five thy father lies;
  Of his bones are coral made:
Those are pearls that were his eyes:
  Nothing of him that doth fade,
But doth suffer a sea-change
Into something rich and strange.
Sea-nymphs hourly ring his knell:
                            ding-dong.
Hark! now I hear them, — ding-dong, bell.

ARIEL'S SONG

(extract from *The Tempest*)

Full fathom five thy father lies;
Of his bones are coral made:
Those are pearls that were his eyes:
Nothing of him that doth fade,
But doth suffer a sea-change
Into something rich and strange.
Sea-nymphs hourly ring his knell:
                              ding-dong.
Hark! now I hear them, – ding-dong, bell.

William Shakespeare

When I was eleven I saw a dead
body on my way home from school.
It was a winter afternoon, getting dark,
and the road to our house led through
a wooded valley where the trees were
thick. A man on a motor-bike came
down, and stopped to tell me that there
was a body by the road just ahead —
heart attack — something like that.

At that point there was a path leading
off the road that I could have taken to
avoid the dead man, but I wanted
to see him, ghoul that I was. So I
went on up the road and there he was,
in the early twilight, looking as if
he'd fallen asleep.

So I went home, impressed and
slightly disappointed.

Philip Pullman

When I was eleven I saw a dead body on my way home from school. It was a winter afternoon, getting dark, and the road to our house led through a wooded valley where the trees were thick. A man on a motorbike came down, and stopped to tell me that there was a body by the road just ahead – heart attack – something like that.

At that point there was a path leading off the road that I could have taken to avoid the dead man, but I wanted to see him, ghoul that I was. So I went on up the road and there he was, in the early twilight, looking as if he'd fallen asleep.

So I went home, unimpressed and slightly disappointed.

PHILIP PULLMAN

The writer communicates and expresses himself with enthusiasm. He is easily motivated, goal-orientated and not distracted from his target. He is helped by his intuition and imagination, which he does not allow to run wild. He is open to new possibilities and only too keen to explore them.

He adapts well to his environment, is sociable and friendly, but will not waste time on trivia. He is also receptive and sensitive, qualities that produce emotions which heighten creativity.

He has spontaneous reactions to events and a need to achieve in a realistic way. He is a genuine and sincere person.

39

MICHEL ROUX

Chef Patron

The Queen of Hearts, She made some tarts,
All on a Summer day:
The Knave of Hearts, he stole those tarts
And took them quite away!

THE QUEEN OF HEARTS

The Queen of Hearts, she made some tarts,
All on a summer day:
The Knave of Hearts, he stole those tarts
And took them quite away!

Lewis Carroll

I chose to be a cook because of my love of food and because I was nearly born in a kitchen!

Going fishing with my father and ferreting for rabits as a child are memories that will never go and always bring a smile to my face.

Michel Roux.

I chose to be a cook because of my love of food and because I was nearly born in a kitchen!

Going fishing with my father and ferreting for rabbits as a child are memories that will never go and always bring a smile to my face.

MICHEL ROUX

MICHEL ROUX

The writer has got where he is by a combination of high aspirations, concentration, courage and energy. He demands a lot of himself, is strong-willed, competitive and determined to succeed. There is single-mindedness in his pursuit of excellence within his chosen field.

However, he is never totally satisfied and inwardly lacks a feeling of complete fulfilment, which presents a challenge and spurs him on to higher achievements.

He organises his work carefully, thinking before acting and also focuses well on the task ahead. He uses his fertile imagination and his good material talents to be creative in his field.

Humour, flair and professional pride, help him cope with his exacting standards and demanding duties.

40

THE EARL OF STOCKTON

Member of the European Parliament

Some One.

Some one came knocking
At my wee, small door;
Some one came knocking,
I'm sure, — sure, — sure;
I listened, I opened,
I looked to left and right,
But nought there was a-stirring
In the still dark night;
Only the busy beetle
Tap-tapping in the wall,
Only from the forest
The screech-owl's call,
Only the cricket whistling
While the dewdrops fall,
So I know not who came knocking,
At all, at all, at all.

Walter de la Mare (1873-1956)

SOME ONE

Some one came knocking
At my wee, small door;
Some one came knocking,
I'm sure – sure – sure;
I listened, I opened,
I looked to left and right,
But nought there was a-stirring
In the still dark night;
Only the busy beetle
Tap-tapping in the wall,
Only from the forest
The screech-owl's call,
Only the cricket whistling
While the dewdrops fall,
So I know not who came knocking,
At all, at all, at all.

Walter de la Mare

237

In 1953 my grandfather had a flat at 90 Piccadilly which overlooked the route of the Coronation procession. We had to arrive the afternoon before and all slept, a little, on the floor in sleeping bags.

Coronation Day dawned grey and wet. But as the troops lining the route took their place, and the bands — one outside the Ritz and another at Hyde Park Corner — started to play, there was plenty to keep us occupied. As we were waiting, there came, without warning, the announcement that Mt. Everest had been climbed by Edmund Hilary and Sherpa Tensing.

Then we all rushed indoors to watch the Queen arrive at Westminster Abbey — on television! It was the first time I had seen television. Just as we saw the Queen and Prince Phillip climb into the gilded coach, the cheers started outside as the head of the procession swung round the corner from St James's Street into Piccadilly.

For hours, or so it seemed, soldiers, sailors and airmen marched past from the U.K. and every country in the Empire and Commonwealth. Prime Ministers and Presidents, Princes, Kings and Queens (not forgetting Queen Salote of Tonga), the great and the good clattered past to the cheers of the crowd.

Until, at the end, came the glittering coach, with the Prince and the Queen, a slight, beautiful and radiant young woman, to whom nearly half the world still owed fealty.

Stockton

In 1953 my grandfather had a flat at 90 Piccadilly which overlooked the route of the Coronation procession. We had to arrive the afternoon before and all slept, a little, on the floor in sleeping bags.

Coronation Day dawned grey and wet. But as the troops lining the route took their place, and the bands – one outside the Ritz and another at Hyde Park Corner – started to play, there was plenty to keep us occupied. As we were waiting, there came without warning, the announcement that Mt. Everest had been climbed by Edmund Hilary and Sherpa Tensing.

Then we all rushed indoors to watch the Queen arrive at Westminster Abbey – on television! It was the first time I had seen television. Just as we saw the Queen and Prince Philip climb into the gilded coach, the cheers started outside as the head of the procession swung round the corner from St James's Street into Piccadilly.

For hours, or so it seemed, soldiers, sailors and airmen marched past from the UK and every country in the Empire and Commonwealth. Prime Ministers and Presidents, Princes, Kings and Queens (not forgetting Queen Salote of Tonga), the great and the good clattered past to the cheers of the crowd.

Until, at the end, came the glittering coach, with the Prince and the Queen, a slight, beautiful and radiant young woman, to whom nearly half the world still owed fealty.

STOCKTON

An evolved personality with a clear, disciplined, orderly and subtle mind, he has harmonious co-ordination of ideas and actions. Towards others he shows a warm sociability and tolerance. He has a respect for conventions and traditional values without compromising either his integrity or independent judgement.

He has a broad and open outlook and a perceptive appreciation of aesthetic style. He carries authority by virtue of his natural personal example and trustworthiness, rather than by aggressive authoritarianism.

Whatever he does is distinguished by a mark of quality.

41

JOANNA TROLLOPE

Novelist

from   Child's Song

I have a fawn from Aden's
                    land,
On leafy buds and berries nurst;
And you shall feed him from
                    your hand,
Though he may start with
                    fear at first.
And I will lead you where
                    he lies
For shelter in the noontide heat;
And you may touch his sleeping
                    eyes,
And feel his little silv'ry feet.

                    Thomas Moore

CHILD'S SONG

I have a fawn from Aden's land,
On leafy buds and berries nurst;
And you shall feed him from your hand,
Though he may start with fear at first.
And I will lead you where he lies
For shelter in the noontide heat;
And you may touch his sleeping eyes,
And feel his little silv'ry feet.

Thomas Moore

I'm a writer because —
chiefly — I believe so much
in the power of story. Stories
are how we learn about
one another, how we
translate ourselves to one
another, how we grow.
I loved stories when I
was tiny: I love them still.
There are few better
questions than, "What
happened next?"

Joanna Trollope

I'm a writer because – chiefly – I believe so much in the power of the story. Stories are how we learn about one another, how we translate ourselves to one another, how we grow. I loved stories when I was tiny: I love them still. There are few better questions than, 'What happened next?'

JOANNA TROLLOPE

This is a shrewd and confident person, in touch with reality. Efficient and resourceful, she makes the most of her opportunities.

Practical and purposeful, she accomplishes what she sets out to do.

She has the ability to see essentials which together with her aestheticism and concern for values impart an air of authority without arrogance or aggression.

Clear thinking and well organised, she has a strong sense of her own autonomy.

42

JEAN URE

Writer

My Shadow

I have a little shadow that goes in and out with
me,
And what can be the use of him is more than
I can see.
He is very very like me from the heels up to
the head;
And I see him jump before me, when I jump
into my bed.

The funniest thing about him is the way he
likes to grow —
Not at all like proper children, which is
always very slow;
For he sometimes shoots up taller like an
india-rubber ball.
And he sometimes gets so little there's none
of him at all.

He hasn't got a notion of how children
ought to play,
And can only make a fool of me in every
sort of way.
He stays so close beside me, he's a coward
you can see;
I'd think shame to stick to nursie as that
shadow sticks to me!

One morning, very early, before the sun
was up,
I rose and found the shining dew on every
buttercup;
But my lazy little shadow, like an arrant
sleepy-head,
Had stayed at home behind me and was
fast asleep in bed.

MY SHADOW

I have a little shadow that goes in and out with me,
And what can be the use of him is more than I can see.
He is very, very like me from the heels up to the head;
And I see him jump before me, when I jump into my bed.

The funniest thing about him is the way he likes to grow –
Not at all like proper children, which is always very slow;
For he sometimes shoots up taller like an india-rubber ball,
And he sometimes gets so little that there's none of him at all.

He hasn't got a notion of how children ought to play,
And can only make a fool of me in every sort of way.
He stays so close beside me, he's a coward you can see;
I'd think shame to stick to nursie as that shadow sticks to me!

One morning, very early, before the sun was up,
I rose and found the shining dew on every buttercup;
But my lazy little shadow, like an arrant sleepy-head,
Had stayed at home behind me and was fast asleep in bed.

Robert Louis Stevenson

A memorable moment from my childhood was when I received the very first
copy of my very first published book.
I was just sixteen & could hardly
believe that this was my book that
I had written! I sat on the stairs
& — surprising reaction — I
giggled. Helplessly! Why, heaven
only knows. Embarrassment, perhaps,
at seeing my name in print...

Jean Ure

A memorable moment from my childhood was when I received the very first copy of my very first published book. I was just sixteen and could hardly believe that this was my book that I had written! I sat on the stairs and – surprising reaction – I giggled. Helplessly! Why, heaven only knows. Embarrassment, perhaps, at seeing my name in print...

JEAN URE

The writer is caring and receptive to others. She has a supple and uncritical mind. An outgoing spontaneity enables her to make quick decisions and have an easy contact with people.

She has a creative imagination with clear judgement and her practical common sense ensures she takes things in her stride.

Her adaptability and flexibility are based upon a sound equilibrium. Her confidence enables her easily to reach her goal without wasted energy.

43

PENNY VINCENZI

Writer

Charity Chadder.

Charity Chadder
Borrowed a ladder,
Leaned it against the moon.
Climbed to the top
Without a stop
On the 31st of June

Brought down every single star
Kept them all in a pickle jar.

                    Charles Causley.

CHARITY CHADDER

Charity Chadder
Borrowed a ladder,
Leaned it against the moon,
Climbed to the top
Without a stop
On the 31st of June,
Brought down every single star,
Kept them all in a pickle jar.

Charles Causley

The memorable moment in my
childhood was also the one that
made me choose my career.

I won an essay competition which
was published in quite a large
circulation regional paper (The
Western Morning News) Seeing
what I'd written transformed into
newsprint was total inspiration &
happiness. I never wanted anything
other than that, professionally
speaking.

Penny Vincenzi

The memorable moment in my childhood was also the one that made me choose my career.

I won an essay competition, which was published in quite a large circulation regional paper (*The Western Morning News*). Seeing what I'd written transformed into newsprint was total, inspirational happiness. I never wanted anything other than that, professionally speaking.

PENNY VINCENZI

The writer has a quick, active, agile mind with good co-ordination between ideas and actions. She is able to see connections between apparently disparate concepts. Her creative flow of ideas can accommodate details without losing sight of the essentials.

There is a tendency towards impulsiveness which she manages to control and transform into results.

She is broad-minded, generous, can be critical but will not bother to bear grudges. She carries authority, is ambitious and is confident enough to override any inner qualms.

44

HARRIET WALTER

Actress

The common cormorant, or shag,
Lays eggs inside a paper bag.
The reason, as you know no doubt,
Is to keep the lightning out.
But what these unobservant birds
Have failed to notice, is that heads
of wandering bears with sticky buns
Steal the bags to hold the crumbs.

THE COMMON CORMORANT

The common cormorant or shag
Lays eggs inside a paper bag.
The reason you will see no doubt
It is to keep the lightning out.
But what those unobservant birds
Have never noticed is that herds
Of wandering bears may come with buns
And steal the bags to hold the crumbs.

Christopher Isherwood

I was staying with an uncle in Holland, and one Sunday he said "We're going to have lunch in Belgium". I had lived all my life in England most of whose borders are sea coast. How could one slip from one country to another over lunch? How could you know where one country ended and another began?

We drove to a country inn having passed a simple border post. It was like stepping from one room of a house into another.

After lunch I wandered off on my own. I came to a small wood of young larch trees and walked through them as though ~~there a~~ through a light green cloud, endless & borderless.

Harriet Walter

I was staying with an uncle in Holland, and one Sunday he said "We're going to have lunch in Belgium." I had lived all my life in England most of whose borders are sea coast. How could one slip from one country to another over lunch? How could you know where one country ended and another began?

We drove to a country inn having passed a simple border post. It was like stepping from one room of a house into another.

After lunch I wandered off on my own. I came to a small wood of young larch trees and walked through them as though through a light green cloud, endless and borderless.

HARRIET WALTER

The writer has an awareness of form and style and aesthetics are important to her.

There is a vulnerability in her nature which she protects by a bold front which could make her difficult to get close to. Any lack of self-assurance is overcome through expression of her artistic talent and her courage in applying it.

She has emotional intensity which gives her a quality of perception. Curiosity and commitment combined with self-control, persistence and patience lead to a perfectionist approach to her work.

Her lyrical imagination and versatility impart a youthful outlook which enables her to meet challenges afresh.

45

AUBERON WAUGH

Journalist

Windy Nights

Whenever the moon and stars are set,
    Whenever the wind is high,
All night long in the dark and wet
    A man goes riding by.
Late in the night when the fires are out,
Why does he gallop and gallop about?

Whenever the trees are crying aloud
    And ships are tossed at sea,
By, on the highway, low and loud,
    By at the gallop goes he.
By at the gallop he goes and then
By he comes back at the gallop again.

ROBERT LOUIS STEVENSON

WINDY NIGHTS

Whenever the moon and stars are set,
   Whenever the wind is high,
All night long in the dark and wet,
   A man goes riding by.
Late in the night when the fires are out,
Why does he gallop and gallop about?

Whenever the trees are crying aloud,
   And ships are tossed at sea,
By, on the highway, low and loud,
   By at the gallop goes he.
By at the gallop he goes, and then
By he comes back at the gallop again.

Robert Louis Stevenson

I was about three or four at the time — in 1942
or 1943, I think — and living with my Grand mother and
about six first cousins when all the children in
the home — a large house, far down in the country near
Dunster, Somerset — were suddenly invited one night
to go on the roof and watch Exeter, just over the
horizon, being bombed by the the Germans. Being ignorant
small children, we clapped and cheered at the excitement
of it, until until told to keep quiet by the grown-ups

Auberon Waugh

Combe Florey, Somerset
August 12 1999

I was about three or four at the time – in 1942 or 1943, I think – and living with my Grandmother and about six first cousins when all the children in the house – a large house, set deep in the country near Dulverton, Somerset – were suddenly united one night to go on the roof and watch Exeter, just over the horizon, being bombed by the Germans. Being ignorant small children, we clapped and cheered at the excitement of it, until told to keep quiet by the grown-ups.

AUBERON WAUGH

This person has an acute, agile mind, critical and discriminating. Underlying an urbane social adaptability and ease of communication, is the dry thinker with a preference for cool detached reflection rather than warm camaraderie.

A tendency to introspection makes him wary of outgoing emotional involvement.

There is a concern for truth and ethics in the abstract so that he might meet eventualities on an everyday level with a superficial humour or pedantry in order to cover deeper concerns and scruples.

He has a perceptive understanding of others although he may not always be sympathetic towards them. He wishes to preserve his objectivity. An elusive mind, he might be difficult to pin down or get to know well.

46

ALAN WHICKER

Broadcaster & Writer

Oh, the grand old Duke of York,
He had ten thousand men;
He marched them up to the top of the hill
And he marched them down again.
And when they were up, they were up,
And when they were down, they were down,
And when they were only halfway up,
They were neither up nor down.

THE GRAND OLD DUKE OF YORK

Oh, the grand old Duke of York,
He had ten thousand men;
He marched them up to the top of the hill
And he marched them down again.
And when they were up, they were up,
And when they were down, they were down,
And when they were only halfway up,
They were neither up nor down.

Traditional

I wanted to write, & to travel.
Hence: Whilst's Well!

A.C. Whilst

I wanted to write, to travel. Hence: *Whicker's World*!

ALAN WHICKER

He has drive, imagination and initiative, with wide interests and social ambition. His energy and certain opportunism enable him to override any inner emotional inhibitions that might get in the way of his goals.

He is understanding of others though he may not show compassion, it is through his cordiality and diplomacy that he is able to get the best out of people.

He might be a difficult person to pin down. Ambition, courage and tenacity all play a part in his achievement of success.

276

47

ANN WIDDECOMBE

Member of Parliament

Faster than fairies, faster than witches
Bridges and horses, hedges and ditches;
And charging along like troops in a battle,
All through the meadows the horses and cattle
All of the sights of the hill and the plain
Fly as thick as driving rain;
And ever again, in the wink of an eye,
Painted stations whistle by.

Here is a child who clambers and scrambles,
All by himself and gathering brambles;
Here is a tramp who stands and gazes;
And there is the green for stringing the daisies!
Here is a cart run away in the road
Lumping along with man and load;
And here is a mill and there is a river:
Each a glimpse and gone forever!

FROM A RAILWAY CARRIAGE

Faster than fairies, faster than witches,
Bridges and houses, hedges and ditches;
And charging along like troops in a battle,
All through the meadows the horses and cattle;
All of the sights of the hill and the plain
Fly as thick as driving rain;
And ever again, in the wink of an eye,
Painted stations whistle by.

Here is a child who clambers and scrambles,
All by himself and gathering brambles;
Here is a tramp who stands and gazes;
And there is the green for stringing the daisies!
Here is a cart run away in the road
Lumping along with man and load;
And here is a mill, and there is a river:
Each a glimpse and gone for ever!

Robert Louis Stevenson

a) The reunion of my family after my parents and I returned from three years in Singapore (my brother and grandmother stayed in England).

b) I like trying to solve the seemingly insoluble.

Ann Widdecombe

(a) The reunion of my family after my parents and I returned from three years in Singapore (my brother and grandmother stayed in England).

(b) I like trying to solve the seemingly insoluble.

ANN WIDDECOMBE

She is a strong individual who relentlessly pursues her tasks. Indefatigable and uncompromising where her principles are concerned, she sees the world in black and white.

Naturally combative, she enjoys the cut and thrust of an argument and has the ability to override her own doubts. She devotes herself single-mindedly to her projects and is proud of the fact. She feels strongly about things. Her thinking is analytical, factual, rapid and decisive, and her judgement can be ruthless and subjective, as well as calculated rather than spontaneous. Combined with her vigour and straightforwardness there is nonetheless a warmth and compassion.

She would be an extremely useful ally and a formidable opponent.

48

JACQUELINE WILSON

Writer of Children's Books

'Over the heather the wet wind blows'

Over the heather the wet wind blows,
I've lice in my tunic and a cold in my nose.

The rain comes pattering out of the sky,
I'm a Wall soldier, I don't know why.

The mist creeps over the hard grey stone,
My girl's in Tungria; I sleep alone.

Aulus goes hanging around her place,
I don't like his manners, I don't like his face.

Piso's a Christian, he worships a fish;
There'd be no kissing if he had his wish.

She gave me a ring but I diced it away,
I want my girl and I want my pay.

When I'm a veteran with only one eye
I shall do nothing but look at the sky.

                              W. H. Auden

'OVER THE HEATHER THE WET WIND BLOWS'

Over the heather the wet wind blows,
I've lice in my tunic and a cold in my nose.

The rain comes pattering out of the sky,
I'm a Wall soldier, I don't know why.

The mist creeps over the hard grey stone,
My girl's in Tungria; I sleep alone.

Aulus goes hanging around her place,
I don't like his manners, I don't like his face.

Piso's a Christian, he worships a fish;
There'd be no kissing if he had his wish.

She gave me a ring but I diced it away,
I want my girl and I want my pay.

When I'm a veteran with only one eye
I shall do nothing but look at the sky.

W. H. Auden

I don't think I 'chose' my particular career (I write children's books). It's almost as if it chose me. I've loved reading since I was five years old and I've also always made up stories and played pretend games. I wrote the way I ate or slept or laughed or cried — it was something I automatically felt I had to do. I still feel that way now.

Jacqueline Wilson

I don't think I 'chose' my particular career (I write children's books). It's almost as if it chose me. I've loved reading since I was five years old and I've also always made up stories and played pretend games. I wrote the way I ate or slept or laughed or cried – it was something I automatically felt I had to do. I still feel that way now.

JACQUELINE WILSON

The writer is a reserved, sensitive person, who observes life realistically and with a detached interest. She is sociable and outgoing, but prefers intimate circles.

She is modest, even rather evasive about herself, as if there were a quiet acceptance of and resignation to life's shortcomings. However these do not interfere with her principles, on which she can take a firm stand; indeed, she has a sense of ethics, duty and responsibility, and is loyal.

Her energy is more mental than physical. She is conscientious and approaches her work in an orderly manner.

She thinks quickly, associating ideas easily. She has imagination, more literary than abstract or pictorial. She likes simplicity and she communicates easily.

She owes her success to persistence, good organisation and discipline, as well as to clarity and firmness of purpose.

COPYRIGHT NOTICES

The publishers would like to acknowledge the following for permission to reproduce copyright material. Every effort has been made to trace copyright holders but in a few cases this has proved impossible. The publishers would be interested to hear from any copyright holders not here acknowledged.